MADELINE

AND THE OLD HOUSE IN PARIS

Story and pictures by
John Bemelmans Marciano

VIKING
An Imprint of Penguin Group (USA) Inc.

To Stella

VIKING
An imprint of Penguin Young Readers Group
Published by the Penguin Group
Penguin Group (USA) Inc.
375 Hudson Street
New York, New York 10014, U.S.A.

USA / Canada / UK / Ireland / Australia / New Zealand / India / South Africa / China
Penguin Books Ltd, Registered Offices: 80 Strand, London WC2R 0RL, England

For more information about the Penguin Group visit www.penguin.com

First published in the United States of America by Viking, an imprint of Penguin Young Readers Group, 2013

Copyright © John Bemelmans Marciano, 2013

LIBRARY OF CONGRESS CATALOGING-IN-PUBLICATION DATA
Marciano, John Bemelmans.
Madeline and the old house in Paris / by John Bemelmans Marciano.
pages cm
Summary: When Lord Cucuface, head of Madeline's school, takes a telescope from the attic
during a surprise inspection, its ghostly owner convinces Madeline to help get it back,
with help from neighbor Pepito and her fellow orphans.
ISBN 978-0-670-78485-1 (hardcover)
[1. Stories in rhyme. 2. Ghosts—Fiction. 3. Stealing—Fiction. 4. Orphans—Fiction.] I. Title.
PZ8.3.M368Mao 2013   [E]—dc23   2012048417

Manufactured in China

1   3   5   7   9   10   8   6   4   2

Set in Bodoni Std
The art for this book was created with gouache and pen and ink on paper.

The publisher does not have any control over and does not assume any responsibility
for author or third-party websites or their content.

ALWAYS LEARNING   PEARSON

In an old house in Paris that was covered with vines
lived twelve little girls in two straight lines.

In another old house that stood next door
lived the son of the Spanish Ambassador.
One afternoon at a quarter to five,
a long black car pulled into the drive.

Wondering who it could possibly be,
Pepito and Madeline ran to see.

It was Lord Cucuface, the sometimes cruel—
and always nosy—head of school.

He had come to make a surprise inspection.

Nothing escaped his skills of detection.

(Save a certain little mouse
who also occupied the house.)

"You can't be too careful with these old houses,
full as they are of termites and louses."
Then Lord Cucuface came before
a thoroughly unfamiliar door,
and asked Miss Clavel what it was for.

"Dear sir, it leads up to the attic,"
said Miss Clavel, her voice emphatic.
"A room that I believe is haunted."
"Rubbish!" the lord said, and completely undaunted,

climbed to an attic that was hot and musty
and filled with old chests that were really quite dusty.
"There are spiders, you see, but nary a ghost!
But what's this?" he said. "Why this is the *most*

splendid telescope I've ever the pleasure
of coming across! Oh what a treasure!"

Cucuface rubbed his hands greedily

and made off with it speedily.

After that they broke their bread

and brushed their teeth

and went to bed.

In the middle of the night
Madeline said, "Something is not right."
She heard the sound of someone moaning,
almost like a ghost was groaning.

The girls all cried, "Look! A ghoul!"
But Madeline was not a fool.

"That's no goblin!" she said. "It's only a brat!"
The boy burst out laughing. Oh, that bad hat!

But the moans went on. In fact they got stronger.
Not even Pepito could laugh any longer.

while the others, afraid, were hesitating.

They crept up the stairs.

Was it a mouse?

A bat?

Or something much scarier than any of that?

It was a ghost!
He cried, "**Woo-hoo!**"

The girls and Pepito cried, "Boohoo."

But Madeline just said,

"Pooh-pooh."

The ghost broke down and started crying.
"Oh, this is even worse than dying!"

Madeline offered him a handkerchief
to stem his flowing ghostly grief.
But his tears fell right on through.
"Monsieur ghost, please tell us, do,
what it is that's troubling you."

"My name is Felix de Lamorte,
and I was born the scientific sort.
Already by the age of seven,
I had mastered the study of the stars in
    heaven.
Proud I was and very glad to be
the first boy admitted to the Academy.
Now comes the woeful part of my story.
I built this house as an observatory
to witness a comet that only nears
the earth every two hundred and
    twenty-one years.
Just as my comet moved into view
I leapt for joy. What is sad but true
is that I forgot I was sitting on a roof.
And my life was over just like that—

"I have haunted this house for years without cease
awaiting the comet so I may rest in peace.
Tomorrow night it finally returns, you see.
But alas! My telescope has been stolen from me!"

Madeline said, "How unfair! How unjust!
We will get it back for you—we must!
Using a wig, these clothes, and even this dust!"

The plan began the very next night
when Miss Clavel turned out the light.

Madeline said, "The coast is clear!"
and gave Pepito the sign to near.

Two girls held a mirror steady
while the rest helped get the costumes ready.

They used a jacket and a scarf of lace
and a piled-up wig and powdered face.

Plus a pair of breeches colored blue
and a buckled high-heeled shoe or two.

They biked to a boat that was waiting below

and rowed their way to this chateau.

"Awake! Awake! Lord Cucuface!
and save yourself from foul disgrace!
You've crossed a line that's awfully fine
by taking what is rightly mine.
The telescope that now I lack
I order you to give me back."

Poor Cucuface, his jaw gone slack,
and halfway to a heart attack,
cried, "Have mercy on a poor old fool!
I was only borrowing it from the school!
It's by the window—don't you see?
Just take it please and leave me be!"

The children seized their prize and then

rowed their way home up the Seine.

Felix was waiting, anxious and glum.

Wouldn't the children ever come?

The door swung open . . .

to reveal to his joy,

the safe return of his best-loved toy.

Felix thanked them with all his heart.

And now begins our final part.

While the rest of the world was soundly sleeping,
a girl and a boy and a ghost were peeping
at a rare and brilliant sight,
a comet streaking through the night.

CANAL